Ghost Stories

Written by Ron Ripley

Edited by Emma Salam

ISBN-13: 978-1540739902
ISBN-10: 1540739902

Thank You and Bonus Novel!

I'd like to take a moment to thank you for your ongoing support. You make this all possible! Also **I would love to send you the full length novel: Sherman's Library Trilogy in 3 formats (MOBI, EPUB and PDF) absolutely free!**

Download Sherman's Library Trilogy in 3 formats, get FREE short stories, and receive future discounts by visiting www.ScareStreet.com/RonRipley

Keeping it spooky,

Ron Ripley

Crowe's Bed and Breakfast

Route 89 was amazing.

The highway cut up through New Hampshire and into Vermont, and it was alive with the bright colors of New England's fall. Derek loved the annual trip up through Connecticut, Massachusetts, New Hampshire, and finally into Vermont. His girlfriend, Wendy, sat in the front passenger seat of his Lexus. She sipped her iced coffee and smiled at him.

"You like it?" he asked.

"Love it," she answered, sighing. "It really is beautiful."

"I love it, too," Derek said with a grin.

"So," she said, "I had an idea."

"What?" he asked, glancing over at her.

"Instead of finding some Holiday Inn or Marriott, why don't we pick out a bed and breakfast?" she said. Derek thought about it for a minute, and then he nodded. Smiling, he said, "Sounds like a great idea. I don't think I've ever stayed in a bed and breakfast in Vermont."

"Mary Ann did last year," she said, "and she and John loved it."

"Do you remember the name of it?" Derek asked.

Wendy shook her head. "I think it was up near Burlington, Vermont. Are we going to go up there?"

"No," he answered. "I'd like to find a place soon. Maybe one with some walking trails. If we can find a good place with a nice view of the Green Mountains."

"Okay," she said happily. "I'll keep my eyes open."

They drove for another twenty minutes in silence, crossed the border into Vermont and continued on their way. "Look," she said suddenly, pointing at a road sign. The faded blue placard looked as though it had stood the New England weather for decades, but the pale white words were still legible.

Crowe's Bed and Breakfast, Exit 3.

"What do you think?" Wendy asked.

"I think we're going to take a look at Crowe's," he replied. She leaned over, gave him a quick kiss and then she settled back in her seat. Fifteen minutes later, the exit came up, and Derek turned off of the highway. At the end of the ramp was another blue sign, equally battered.

Mason, Vermont, 4 miles. Crowe's Bed and Breakfast, 4.1 miles.

"Looks like we're going to Mason, Vermont," Derek said, chuckling. He felt giddy, excited. In his stomach, butterflies flew, the same feeling he always had with a new girlfriend. He turned left towards the bed and breakfast and in a short time they passed a small marker which read, *Mason, Vermont, Established 1797.* Barely a hundred yards up was a tall, nearly overgrown sign decorated with a painted black crow.

Crowe's Bed and Breakfast, accompanied by a drawn hand which pointed the way down a narrow road. A pair of tall, black lamps marked the entrance and Derek signaled before he turned in. Ancient trees ran along the length of the cracked asphalt and their huge boughs locked over the passage to create a thick canopy of brightly colored leaves. The road curved ever so slightly to the left, and then it widened suddenly to reveal a beautiful, grand Victorian with a large farmer's porch. Chrysanthemums of various colors hung in wicker baskets from the trim work and all of the windows seemed to glow from lights within the house. "It's beautiful," Wendy said softly.

Derek could only nod his head in agreement. Several cars were parked off to the left of the building, and Derek was impressed. One of them looked like it was an early Mustang, painted metallic green and in almost mint condition. One was a wood-paneled station wagon, and a third was a silver, 1980's Jaguar.

"Wow," he said, pulling in beside the wagon. "These cars are awesome." Wendy laughed and shook her head. "Let's worry about getting a room before you go around and start harassing the other guests about their cars." "Sounds good to me," Derek said, grinning.

He turned off the engine and got out of the car. Wendy came around to him as he stretched and tried to work the kinks out of his body.

"Feeling old?" she asked teasingly.

"Almost," Derek said, smiling. "Almost."

"Well," Wendy said, stepping in close and kissing his neck. "I'll help you forget those aches and pains later."

"Promises, promises," Derek said. He titled his head slightly to kiss her, but Wendy slipped away with a laugh.

"Do you want to bring the bags in?" she asked.

"No," he said, stifling a yawn. "Let's make sure they've got a room first." Wendy nodded and held out her hand. Derek took hold of it loosely and together they followed a brick walkway to the porch. They climbed the stairs and saw an "Open" sign in the glass of the front door.

As they entered the bed and breakfast, a bright, cheerful bell rang above them and an older woman, tall and elegant, appeared from a side door. A small brass plate set above the lintel read, *Office*.

"Good afternoon," the woman said, brushing a strand of silver hair behind her ear. Her full-length, gray skirt brushed across the polished wood of the floor, and she wore a white blouse beneath a red wrap. Her lips were a darker shade of red, and she looked to be in her sixties, and stunningly attractive. She smiled at them, her teeth a brilliant white and slightly crooked.

"Hello," Derek and Wendy said in unison.

"We're wondering," Derek continued, "if you have any rooms available?"

"Of course," the woman said, her smile widening. "We always have rooms ready for guests."

"Oh good," Wendy said. "We were worried we'd be out of luck, what with the cars in the parking lot." The woman's smile faltered and then became strong again.

"Oh, those. No. Those cars don't belong to anyone in particular. They've all been left here."

"Really?" Derek asked, surprised. "They're beautiful." The woman shrugged, pulled her knitted wrap around her tighter and said, "To some. My husband used to think so as well."

"Used to?" Derek asked, grunting as Wendy shot him a look and nudged him in the side with an elbow.

"I'm a widow," the woman said. "My Henry passed away a long time ago. But let's not worry about such things. If you'll follow me into the office, we can get the paperwork settled and get you into your room. I'm afraid I've already served lunch, but there are plenty of cold cuts and fresh bread. I also made a large pitcher of iced tea if either of you are interested.

"Of course," she continued as she walked around a large, dark wood desk and sat down, "I am always happy to put coffee on as well. Dinner, if you stay, will be served at six. Now, please, sit down."

She gestured to a pair of small side chairs, and Derek and Wendy did so. For a moment, the woman got some papers out of a drawer and a pair of reading glasses from another. She set the pearl colored frames on her delicate nose and murmured to herself as she found a fountain pen.

"Ah," she said, smiling, "here we are."

She slid the papers across to Derek and said, "This is the standard agreement, thirty-five dollars per person, per night, with all meals included. If there's anything you or your wife would like to eat in particular, please, just let me know and I'll see if I have the ingredients." Derek was stunned at the low price and nearly said so. Wendy, however, didn't hesitate. "My husband's tired. We drove up from New York. Your price sounds excellent. Are you sure you don't want more?"

"No," the woman smiled. "My Henry left me quite comfortable. I run the house mostly for the company. But, I thank you."

Wendy nodded, picked up the fountain pen and filled out the paperwork as if they were married, and handed it all back to the woman.

"Excellent," she said. "Now, my name is Mrs. Fallow. Your room is number five, which is up the stairs and to the right. I can be reached anytime of the day or night, so please, don't hesitate to ask. Payment will be due when you check out."

"Wonderful," Wendy said, standing up.

"Yes, wonderful," Derek repeated as he got to his feet. Mrs. Fallow took a key off of a hook on the left wall and handed it to Wendy.

"Thank you," Wendy said, smiling.

"No, no, thank you," Mrs. Fallow said, returning the smile. "I will see you at breakfast, which is served between seven and ten in the morning."

Derek and Wendy nodded, and he followed her out of the office. He started to turn towards the front door, but Wendy tugged on his arm.

"Come on," she said, shaking the key. "Let's check out the room!"

"Okay," he said, grinning.

They went up the broad stairs and to the room. Number five was locked, but Wendy quickly had it open. A large bed dominated the center of the room, and a pair of matching chairs stood off to the left. On the right, a small door opened to an equally tiny bathroom, and a pair of tall windows looked out over a long, narrow pasture.

"This is beautiful," Wendy said, stepping forward to look out at the landscape.

"It is," Derek agreed. He closed the door and saw a long bureau against the wall. As he went to toss his keys onto the bureau's white marble top, he paused. Three sets of keys were already there. One was to a Jaguar.

"Hey hon," Wendy said. He looked over at her and saw she had opened a closet door.

"Check this out," she said, nodding to the interior. Derek dropped his keys besides the others and joined her. Inside of the closet were five jackets. They were of various ages and styles, and each was hung neatly on a wooden hanger.

"Weird," he said. "There are keys over on the bureau, too."

Wendy looked over, frowned and shook her head. "It is weird."

She took out a pair of hangers and handed one to Derek. He accepted it and shrugged off his coat. A moment later, he hung it up in the closet and Wendy did the same with hers. She closed the door and shook her head again.

"So," Derek said, smiling and putting his hands on her waist. "Do you want to do anything before we get the bags out of the car?"

"Maybe," she said with a wink. Derek leaned in for a kiss and stopped as a loud crash sounded outside of the door. He jerked up and looked over his shoulder.

"What do you think it was?" Wendy asked. He started to answer, but a scream cut him off. "Henry!" a woman shrieked. *Mrs. Fallow*? Derek thought. He glanced at Wendy, and she mouthed the woman's name. Derek nodded.

"Henry," Mrs. Fallow said, this time right outside the door. "I know you're in there, Henry. I know *she's* with you. Don't think I don't. I can *smell* the little trollop."

"What?" Wendy whispered. Derek shook his head, utterly confused.

"Stay in there, Henry," Mrs. Fallow whispered. "Stay in there with her."

A dark liquid suddenly seeped under the door and the room filled with the foul stench of gasoline. "Oh Jesus," Derek managed to say, and then fire exploded into the room. The walls burst into flames, and he shouted, "The windows!"

Wendy spun around out of his arms, ran to the nearest window and went to throw the sash up. "No!" she screamed. Derek reached her side and saw the reason for her despair. The sash was nailed shut. As was the other window's. Smoke billowed out from the walls as Derek and Wendy coughed, their breath stolen from them. He staggered to a chair, grabbed hold of it and went to lift it only to lose his grip and fall backward. On the floor, he rolled onto his stomach and saw the feet of the chairs were nailed as firmly to the wood planks as the window's sash was to the sill.

Wendy smashed out several of the panes, but the fresh air only fed the fire. An explosion from behind them slammed her into the window. She reeled and collapsed. Blood spilled from a huge gash on her forehead and her eyelids fluttered.

"Wendy," Derek said, coughing. He crawled towards her, pulled her into his arms and tried to get to his feet. But the smoke swept over him, blinded him, and dragged him back to the floor.

6

***

State Trooper Dan Waters turned at the old Mason road and slowed his cruiser down at the entrance to Crowe's Bed and Breakfast. The leaves and branches which had covered the entrance early in the morning were disturbed. Fresh tire tracks cut through them. Dan frowned, put on his searchlight and his high-beams, and called in his position.

When dispatch confirmed their receipt of the call, he eased the car onto the old driveway. Soon his lights illuminated the cars. And a new one too. A black, 2014 Lexus sedan with New York tags. He pulled up behind it, jotted down the information, and then he swept his searchlight across the bed and breakfast. The old, burned remains of the old Victorian stood out starkly against the elms and oaks which surrounded it. Since 1967, the place had been a magnet for ghost hunters.

Nothing pulls 'em in like a double murder-suicide, Dan thought. He considered getting out and trying to find whoever had come in the Lexus. *Nope,* he decided, turning the cruiser around and heading back to Mason Road. *Place scares the hell out of me.* For a moment, Dan thought he could smell burnt wood. He shook his head.

Now you're imaging things, he told himself and he focused on the cup of coffee he was going to get up at the gas station off exit 19.

* * *

The Dog Tracker

Adam stood outside of the hen house and looked at the carnage. Feathers and blood littered the yard around the long wooden structure. Dozens of shell-shocked hens stood around Adam. The rooster, his strut stolen by the chaos of the early morning, wandered around, mute. A few pecked at Adam's feet, impatient for the feed he carried.

Adam walked off to one side, scattered the chicken food about, and once the birds had flocked to it, he went back to the scene of destruction. He dropped down to his haunches and looked close at a single, large paw print stamped in blood churned earth.

A Dog, Adam thought. He straightened up. *Damned big one too.* He checked the birds' water and then he went back to the house. Michelle was in the kitchen by the stove. She was holding a polishing cloth in her hand, and she paused and smiled at him. The smile quickly dropped away. "What's wrong?"

"A dog got into the hen house this morning," he said, putting the feed bucket down by the back door. "Must have happened when we went out for our walk."

"Not coyotes?" she asked.

He shook his head. "There's a single track out there, and it's huge. Too big for a coyote."

"No one around here has a big dog," Michelle said, brushing a lock of black hair back behind her ear.

"Must be feral," Adam said. "Maybe living in Mason."

"You going to call animal control over in Rye?" she asked.

"No," he said. "They won't do anything. People don't care if a few chickens get taken. I'll track it as far as I can, see if I can take care of the damned thing myself."

"Okay," she said. "Just bring your phone. I can drive in and pick you up rather than having you walk all the way back."

"Thanks, Sweetheart," Adam said. He stepped close, gave her a quick kiss on the mouth and then left for the family room. From the gun cabinet, he took out his pump action shotgun, a box of shells, and he grabbed his phone off of the charger. He quietly loaded the weapon, and tucked the box into a pocket of his jacket along with his phone.

Adam cradled the shotgun in the crook of his arm and left the room. Michelle was back at the stove, and he couldn't see what she was so focused on. The appliance positively glowed as the warm morning light streamed in through the window over the sink.

"Be safe," she said as Adam went to the back door. "And call when you can."

"I will," he replied, and he left the house.

Quick steps brought him to the back of the hen house, and he saw a hole in the chicken wire. On the other side, he found another paw print on a small game trail opposite of the break. Adam focused on the path before him, and he started to track the dog.

Broken branches. Disturbed leaves. The occasional mark of a paw. A bit of fur.

And as he had thought, the trail continued on northwest, toward Mason.

Soon, he caught sight of a brick chimney. It stood alone, without a house around it. The remains of a foundation protruded from the earth.

In less than five minutes, he found himself on an asphalt road, much of it hidden by fallen leaves and broken branches. The remnants of houses appeared on either side, and occasional side roads branched off.

But the tracks of the dog continued on.

The trail was easy to follow, leaves kicked up as the dog had made its way straight down the center of the road.

Finally, Adam came to Main Street, and he paused.

The stretch of road frightened him.

Only a dozen or so buildings populated the street, and none of them looked as though they belonged in a horror movie, but there was something off about the structures. Some of the windows were broken. Some were boarded up. All of them were faded, the signs difficult to read. It was the total abandonment. The *emptiness* of the town.

People had left. No one really knew why, and former residents were hard-pressed to admit they had ever lived in

Mason. Like any town or city, it had its morbid spots. The old Crowe Bed and Breakfast. The Mason Cemetery. Hell, someone had even told him once the library was haunted. Adam scoffed at the memory of the story, and he shook his head.

The dog suddenly trotted out between the old gas station and the hardware store. A great big Dobermann. Lean and dark, the ears clipped, and the tail cropped. The dog swung its long muzzle towards him, and Adam could see the dried blood on the animal's snout.

"I see you," Adam murmured. He swung the shotgun up to his shoulder, pumped a round into the chamber, and fired even as the dog broke into a sprint. The shot missed, but not by much. The solid round hammered into a telephone pole and bit out a chunk of treated wood. He followed the dog and got ready to pull the trigger, but it leaped through the empty window of a building.

"Damn it," Adam spat. He lowered the shotgun slightly and walked forward. He angled towards the building and caught a glimpse of an old sign over the door.

Mason Montessori School for Gifted Children.

Adam sneered at the idea of gifted children, kept a wary eye on the window the dog had jumped through, and tried the handle. The door was unlocked. He let himself in and stood in a room with small chairs and small desks. Empty shelves, built at the perfect height for young children, lined the walls. Faded letters and numbers clung everywhere, and spider webs filled the corners of the ceiling. Leaves lay scattered about the tiled floor, and a few bones of various ages were intermingled. It was the dog's den.

But where's the dog? Adam thought. A broken door, which hung haphazardly from the top hinge, was the only other way out of the room. Adam smiled to himself and approached it cautiously. He heard a soft whine, followed by several scratches, and he knew he had the dog. With a deep breath, he kept the shotgun steady and pushed the door open. The room beyond was dimly lit. The light from the front of the building barely breached the darkness. At the edge of his vision, Adam saw the dog. It slipped into a darker shadow to the right and whined again.

"I've got you," he whispered, pumping a round into the chamber.

"What are you doing?" a small voice asked. Adam paused, shocked. *The dog's not alone?* The words had issued from the same place the dog had disappeared into.

"What are you doing?" the voice asked again.

It was a little boy. Maybe even a girl. Adam couldn't be sure. He lowered the shotgun, glad he hadn't just fired into the shadow.

"I'm chasing a dog," Adam said, squinting and trying to see. All he could make out was the dog. It sat quietly.

"He's my dog," the child said.

"Your dog ate my chickens, son," Adam said.

"I'm a girl," the child said angrily. "My name's Becca."

"Well, Becca, your dog," Adam began.

"Achilles," she said.

"What?" Adam asked.

"His name is Achilles."

"Well," Adam said, trying not to be frustrated. "Achilles ate my chickens."

"He was hungry."

Adam rolled his eyes. "Doesn't matter, Becca. Can't be eating my chickens. And besides. You two can't be out here. Do your parents know where you are? Did you run away?"

"He was hungry," she said again. *Jesus help me,* Adam thought, sighing. "Becca, did you run away from home?"

"I am home," she said.

"Becca," Adam said.

"Achilles is my dog. We're home. He was hungry," she said. Then, in an angry voice, she asked, "Were you going to shoot my dog?"

"He killed my chickens," Adam said defensively. "Now listen, I'm going to call the police. They'll come and get you."

"What about Achilles?" she asked.

"They'll take him to the shelter," he answered.

"What's the shelter? Is it like the pound?" she asked.

"Yes," Adam said.

"No."

"You can't say 'no,' Becca," Adam said angrily. He took his phone out of his pocket, hit the flashlight app and held it up to look at her.

Achilles sat perfectly still, his ears up and his eyes trained on Adam. There was no girl.

"Put the flashlight away," Becca said, her voice coming from beside the dog.

Adam swallowed nervously and looked around. Then, down by the dog's right paw, he saw a small, stuffed bear. The toy was dressed in a faded pink tutu, and it wore a tiara. Its fur was matted, and one of its glass eyes was gone.

"I said put it away!" she screamed. The phone went dead in his hand. Adam blinked, tried to focus and attempted to turn the flashlight app back on. It didn't work. The dog whined.

"You tried to hurt Achilles," Becca said, and her voice was closer. Adam dropped his phone and held onto his shotgun with both hands.

"And you want to have him put in the pound," she hissed. She was behind him.

Adam spun around and something hit him in the small of his back. He stumbled, hit the wall and fell. But he didn't let go of the shotgun. He scrambled into a seated position and kept the weapon in front of him. Small hands closed over his. The feeling was terrible, ice-penetrating his flesh, digging deep into his bones. It seemed as though his fingernails were going to be ripped out at their roots. He tried to shake the hands away, but he couldn't even let go of the shotgun. And then the dog was there. Adam could feel Achilles' breath on his face and smell the rot of old flesh caught between the dog's teeth. A low, primal growl settled in the dog's throat and raised goose bumps along Adam's arms.

"You wanted to kill my dog," Becca whispered. "You're not nice. I bet you'd try and steal my Princess Bear too. You're mean. *Mean.*"

The shotgun moved in his hands. The barrel rose up, and he fought it, tried to push back. He couldn't. Becca was too strong. A scream erupted from his throat as she continued to bring the weapon up and his trigger finger broke. His wrist was twisted out of its socket, and so was his elbow, and then his shoulder. He gagged on the pain and writhed against the wall. She wouldn't let him go. The cold steel barrel of the shotgun slammed into his right eye and then he shrieked as she continued to push it back. The orb was forced out of the socket. His arm twisted beyond any semblance of normalcy.

"You were going to hurt my dog," Becca whispered. "My dog."

Adam felt her small, dead hand push down on his mangled finger. He looked over and saw a young girl, perhaps seven or eight. She was deathly pale, her eyes empty and black. Her blue lips were pressed tightly together and she was thin. Painfully so.

"My *dog,*" she hissed.

She started to tighten his finger on the trigger, and Adam realized, with the way she had twisted his arm, it would look as though he had committed suicide.

And then the shotgun fired.

* * *

The Treasure Hunter

Jack Matthews specialized in fine antiques, artwork, and estate jewelry. Many people saw him around at various estate sales, auctions, and the occasional flea market. Nobody ever witnessed him purchasing estate jewelry, however. Because Jack didn't buy it.

He stole it.

Jack was an accomplished grave robber. He sat in his Jeep Wrangler, parked on an old logging road, half a mile outside of Mason. The driver's side window was slightly open, just enough to let the smoke from his thin Turkish cigar escape into the warm summer air. It was early in the morning, and, like clockwork, the State trooper who patrolled the ghost town's main road, cruised through. Jack had seen the officer. The young man had been speaking into a cellphone and far more intent on his conversation than on anything else around him. Which was perfect for Jack. The trooper wouldn't make another pass through Mason until eight hours later. Jack had plenty of time to prospect.

He placed a well-thumbed copy of *A Guide to New England Birds*, on the passenger seat, and he double checked his work bag. A collapsible shovel, coveralls, some water as well as a bag of trail mix, and a pair of high-powered binoculars. Jack doubted anyone would even stop by, but it paid to have a cover story handy.

In Jack's experience, the dead didn't care about their rest being disturbed, but it sure as hell irritated the living. Jack got out of the Jeep, locked the doors and put the keys away in his bag. He slipped his arms through the straps and started off on a roughly straight line towards what had once been the center of Mason. He moved along quickly. The sooner he was done, the better he would feel.

There was always the chance of being discovered, and Jack didn't want to push his luck. Within five minutes, he had cut through the woods and reached a small side neighborhood with abandoned houses. He ignored these and continued on his way.

Five more minutes of fast walking put him at the Mason cemetery, and at the old iron-gate, he paused to look around. There were a few hundred headstones within the protected confines of an old stone wall. Tall pines grew up along the edges, their boughs heavy as they hung over the headstones. At the far back corner of the cemetery stood a decrepit, single story house. A caretaker's building. The paint had long flecked off the shuttered windows and the closed door. Holes stood out starkly in the old roof, and the brick walls looked as though they might crumble into dust. Jack smiled.

The place was perfect. Absolutely abandoned. And his research had told him how the last burial had taken place in 1964. The first of them, however, had taken place in the late seventeen hundreds. Yet those didn't hold any interest for Jack.

He wanted the Victorians and the Edwardians. The mid to late nineteenth century and the early twentieth. The people who would have been buried with their jewels and their gold. Jack knew what years to look for. Practice had helped him to be perfect.

With a happy whistle, Jack slipped through the gate and made his way to the center of the cemetery. He looked for the obelisks and urns which would mark the Victorians, and he found them. Dozens of them. He sighed with pleasure and set his bag down. He walked carefully from headstone to headstone until he found one with promise.

"Mary Lee Locke, Beloved Wife and Mother," Jack read aloud. Mary Locke had died when she was sixty-seven. Children would have been married. Her jewelry would be with her.

Jack hummed to himself as he went back to his bag. He put on his coveralls, took a drink of water, a handful of trail mix, and assembled the shovel. Soon he was back at Mary's grave, and he started to dig.

He made sure to pace himself, and to carefully set aside the top layer of sod. He dug steadily and cautiously. With age, the top of the coffin would have weakened. Several times he had crashed through rotten wood and then spent hours cleaning the remnants of flesh, bone and clothing from his boots.

After a short while, he was roughly a foot down. He paused to give his back a rest. A loud, creak sounded, and Jack turned to look around. One of the shutters on the caretaker's house had come free. It swung lazily in and out, and with each movement one of the hinges screamed out in protest. Jack chuckled and turned back to his work.

Only a few minutes had passed before he heard a different noise. A loud, almost groan which echoed off the stones and filled the quiet air. Jack straightened up and looked at the building again. The door was open. And not a little, but open completely, so it rested against the brick wall.

What the hell? Jack thought. *Is there someone living in there?* Fear suddenly flooded through him, and Jack got out of the large hole he had dug. He gripped the handle of the shovel tightly and took a nervous step towards the house.

"Hello?" Jack called out.

No one answered him. He walked a little closer. "Hello," Jack said again. "Is there anyone there?" The open shutter closed with a bang and Jack nearly jumped. *I have to lock those,* he thought. *If I don't, they're going to drive me crazy.*

He lowered the shovel slightly and walked boldly forward. Once at the door, he stopped and peered in.

A small desk stood against the far wall. Above it, hung a faded and illegible calendar. Off to the right, a variety of shovels rested against the wall. On the left, were a table and a pair of chairs. An old radio stood on it, the antenna straight up. No one was in the house. No one had been in the building for a terribly long time as far as Jack could tell. The shutter opened and banged, and Jack jumped in fear. *Yeah, this needs to stop,* he thought angrily. He dropped the shovel onto the table, went to the window and pulled the shutter in. With quick movements, he found the iron latches and locked the old wood in place.

He took a step back, grinned and wiped the dust and dirt off his hands and onto his coveralls. Jack turned to pick up his shovel and froze, petrified into stillness. An old man sat at the table. He wore a knit cap and a flannel shirt. His face was thin and haggard. The eyes, blue and cold. Narrow, pale lips were pressed close together, and Jack realized he could almost see through the man. The stranger's edges were fuzzy, as though they weren't quite finished.

He's a ghost, isn't he? Jack thought. *Yes. He has to be.* And then he realized the dead man's pale blue eyes were fixed on him.

"What are you doing here?" Jack asked. He tried to control the fear which threatened to overwhelm him. A look of surprise flashed across the ghost's face, and then he smiled. "Oh no, I'm the one who's to ask you. And so I do, what are *you* doing here?"

"I work for the State," Jack lied, his heart beating spasmodically. "I'm here to check on the graves."

The ghost laughed and shook his head. "Ah, you do lie well, whoever you are. But it makes no difference if you are who you say you are, or simply another thief. Both results are the same."

Jack took a cautious step towards the exit and the dead man flashed him a grin of yellowed and broken teeth. The door slammed shut.

"You just arrived, young man," the ghost said softly. "Why would you wish to leave so soon?"

Panic climbed into Jack's throat in the form of a scream, and he swallowed convulsively to keep it down.

"I have to go," Jack said, his words coming out in a hoarse whisper.

"Oh no," the dead man said, standing up. "I don't think you do. You're going to stay awhile."

Jack lost the battle with his fear. The scream he had struggled to contain ripped free. The sound of his own voice punished his own ears, and Jack turned so quickly he stumbled and fell to his knees. He didn't try to get up. Instead, he scurried forward on all fours to the door. He reached the old wood, grabbed hold of the black metal handle and pulled himself up. A whistle came from behind him, and something heavy struck him in the back of the head. Stars exploded in front of Jack's eyes, and he slipped down the door to lay crumpled on the dirt floor. Darkness lapped over his vision with all of the calm, cold detachment of the sea.

A bitterly cold hand grasped him by the back of the neck, and the door sprang open. Jack's limbs hung loosely, and he found himself dragged out into the daylight. The darkness parted, he saw the graveyard, and then his sight disappeared again. He felt the rough ground and the cool grass beneath him. Then, through the darkness, Jack could smell fresh earth. His sight returned. Jack blinked and felt himself slide down, and he realized he was in Mary's grave.

Oh no, Jack thought, trying to move. *Oh, this can't be happening. No way.*

But his limbs didn't respond. Only his eyes flickered from left to right frantically. He looked up at the pale blue sky. An occasional cloud passed through his line of sight, but nothing more. The dead man stepped into Jack's view and squatted down. He smiled.

"I suppose," the ghost said, "you think something mundane as being buried alive is going to happen to you."

Jack didn't answer. He couldn't.

"Oh, don't worry," the dead man said. "I can see it in your eyes. But don't worry, don't worry. I'm not going to do such a thing to you. No. Not me."

The ghost stood up and stepped away. A moment later, a shovel full of dirt was thrown into the hole. It landed lightly on Jack's legs, and more of the dark, rich earth followed. Soon, every part of Jack was covered, save for his head. Occasionally the ghost would reach in, brush some wayward dirt away from Jack's face. Then the burying began again.

Within a short while, as Jack's thoughts raced with panic, only his face remained free. The ghost brought forth the turf Jack had so carefully set aside, and fit it neatly over the fresh earth. Jack hyperventilated as the grass was tucked neatly around his face.

The dead man returned. Once more, he squatted down beside the grave and smiled at Jack.

"See," the ghost said. "You were afraid I was going to cover your face up, too, weren't you?"

Jack remained silent.

"No," the dead man said happily. "You won't suffocate to death. Nor will the weight crush you. Not enough of it. But you'll starve to death. Course bugs and animals might get at your face first."

The ghost leaned forward, the smile on his face vanished.

"Perhaps," he said softly, "you'll understand why it's wrong to rob the dead."

The dead man stood and left. Jack was alone. Tears welled up in his eyes as he looked into the sky and felt the first ant run across his face. The insect's legs tickled his lips, and Jack tried desperately to scream as it slipped into his mouth.

* * *

The Rosary

Connor looked through the haze of tobacco smoke from his pipe at the morning light as it crested the horizon. A flock of turkeys moved through the tall grass, their dark feathers flush with the sun's glow. The pair of toms that watched over the hens stood a little distance away from their harem, tails spread and waddles bright red.

Connor grinned, tipped his hat in salute to the birds and stepped off his porch. His knees and hips ached. Decades of farm work had punished his joints, worn down his muscles and beat upon his back.

Over the years, he had sold off bits and pieces of the land. Young folk, hell bent to make money on corn when you couldn't even give it away. Connor shook his head, settled his pipe firmly in his mouth and put his hands in the pockets of his work-worn overalls. His feet followed the same path he had tread every morning for thirty-seven years. Sixty-two steps from the back porch to the right wall. Gray stones piled over generations to mark the pastures and the fields.

He reached it after a few moments and turned left. With the wall on his right, he followed it along the acres he still owned. Connor knew where each stone should be, the placement of every rock. Some, he had put up with his sons. Some, alone. And others, with his father, and his grandfather. He knew the wall intimately, and it helped him prepare for each day. When he reached the far corner, he came to a stop. Just beyond the wall, was the new road. Yet at the junction of stones, Connor found one had fallen, a rare, yet not unseen occurrence.

The stone was a roughly triangular piece of granite which glinted in the morning sun. Connor grimaced at the pain in his hips as he squatted and picked up the stone. He went to replace it and paused. In the granite's former seat, he found a rosary. Connor gently removed the religious item. Behind it, was a small envelope sealed in wax paper, and Connor withdrew it as well. With a shake of his head, he properly put the stone back in its place. He straightened up, winced at the audible 'pop' from his right leg, and held the rosary up to the morning light.

The beads were a pale gray, connected by delicate links of steel. The crucifix was of steel as well, the image of Christ potent and powerful. His suffering nearly unbearable to behold.

How did you get here? Connor wondered, turning the crucifix over. On the back, he found an inscription.

Jonathan, come home to me safely. Mother. October 9, 1943.

Connor held the rosary in his hands and looked at it.

Why were you in my wall? He thought. Once more, he read the inscription.

Jonathan, come home to me safely. Mother. October 9, 1943.

Jonathan.

1943.

Connor's eyes widened. *Jonathan Farley,* Connor realized. He remembered the funeral. He had been a boy and the Farley's had lived on the next farm over. Jonathan had died somewhere in the Pacific. He had been killed by the Japanese.

But, why were you in my wall? he wondered as he held the rosary in one hand and opened the envelope.

It contained a letter written on one side of heavy card stock, and was no bigger than a postcard. The penmanship was neat and precise.

To Whom It May Concern,

I have placed this rosary, which belonged to my son, Jonathan, here in this wall. This part of the field was his favorite, and I always thought it a shame he had died before ever seeing the sunrise from it again. I have taken the liberty of placing his crucifix here in hopes that his spirit will be at peace. If you find it, I ask you to leave it. I am certain it would make his troubled soul happy.

Mary Farley, June, 1945

Connor read the letter again and shook his head. *Has it been here for sixty years?*

He sighed and put it into his breast pocket, along with the rosary.

The wall's mine, Connor thought stubbornly. He shook his head and turned to the left. The beads were surprisingly warm against his chest, as though they had been in the sun and not behind the rock. One of the toms looked up, watched him for a moment, then the turkey returned to the concerns of hens, food and predators. Connor smiled, finished his walk, and returned to his house.

He poured himself a glass of water, carried it into the den with him and sat down to read the morning newspaper. There was little Connor considered newsworthy, but, like his walk, the paper was part of his daily ritual. As was the water, which he drank slowly.

Soon, he finished the paper, closed his eyes and thought about the stories he had read. Heroin arrests in Nashua. A bank robbery in Nashua. The president of the local Chamber of Commerce in a bit of situation because of lurid emails sent to the coach of the Hollis High School's cheer squad. *Nothing new,* Connor thought.

The heat of the rosary in his pocket flared up, and his eyes snapped open. It felt as though the beads were made of fire. He snarled at the sudden pain, dug the beads out and held them in his hands. Beads and steel and crucifix were cool to the touch.

For a moment, he looked at them with worry and wondered if dementia had decided to rear its ugly head. It had with Janice, and now he had to visit his wife in the nursing home. The illness had made her too difficult to handle. Connor sighed, looked at the rosary and a memory flashed before him. The funeral of Jonathan Farley, the whispers. Jonathan's brothers speaking of the horrific deeds their older brother had committed. The human skulls he had mailed home. The rambling letters speaking of the atrocities he had witnessed and had participated in. The war had claimed Jonathan in more ways than one.

I doubt looking at the sunrise would have eased his soul, Connor thought, and then he set it down on the coffee table. He stood up, finished the last bit of water and returned to the kitchen to refill the glass. His steps were slow, and he worried again about dementia. He reached the sink and froze as something crashed in the den. Connor stood immobile, one hand above the faucet, the other wrapped around the glass. A soft, low noise reached his ears, and Connor stiffened. *Someone's crying,* he realized. *Someone's in my house.*

He put the glass down, opened the silverware drawer and pulled out the small, snub-nosed revolver he kept tucked in the back of it. He reached a little further back, found the box of shells and quickly loaded the weapon. With a snap of his wrist, Connor locked the cylinder in place, cocked the hammer back and held the pistol out protectively.

He carefully walked back to the den. He tried to remember if he had heard anyone on the front porch, or if he had foolishly left any of the windows or doors on the first floor unlocked. Nothing came to mind. The sound of the person's sobs grew louder, and Connor's heart beat quicker.

A few steps away from the doorway into the den, he stopped and took several long, deep breaths. He forced himself to calm down, inhaled through his nose one last time, exhaled, and quickly went in. A man knelt in front of the couch with his back to Connor. Fine sand was strewn about the room, as though an entire section of beach had been transported into the house. The man was in the center of the sand, and Connor realized the stranger wore a faded, olive drab uniform.

"Who are you?" Connor demanded, keeping the pistol up and pointing at the young man's back. The stranger's shoulders shook, his head bowed. Connor worked his jaw nervously, tried to figure out how the young man had gotten in, how *sand* had gotten in.

"Who are you?" Connor snapped. The stranger's head lifted up, and he sniffed loudly.

"Did you see what they made me do?" the man whispered.

"Son," Connor said, "I've got a gun pointed at your back. Unless you want me to put a bullet in you, you best answer my question."

"Did you see what they made me do?" the sobbing man repeated.

"Son," Connor said again, and the gun went off in his hand. He staggered back, surprised, shocked and horrified. He looked at the man and waited in fear for the blood to appear on the stranger's back.

Nothing happened.

Nothing at all.

Then something finally did.

Connor could suddenly see through the disturbed stranger. He could see the couch. Connor saw the bullet hole in the piece of furniture. The man stood up and turned around. He was a handsome, young man, perhaps eighteen or nineteen years old. He was also stunned, as though he couldn't quite believe what had happened. He was Jonathan Farley. The stunned look slipped away, replaced by fierce anger.

"I wanted to watch the sunrise. And they came over. Hundreds of them," he hissed "Look at what they made me do."

And it was then Connor saw what Jonathan had in his hands. In the left hand, was a huge fighting knife. The steel was dark red with blood. Looped around the hand and the weapon's hilt was the rosary Connor had found in the wall. The young man's right hand tightly gripped the short, dark hair of a severed head. Dead eyes looked up, the mouth was slightly agape, and blood dripped from the ragged strips of skin around the neck. Each crimson jewel struck the nearly white sand and vanished.

"Look what they made me do," Jonathan said. He held the head up higher for Connor to see better. Connor couldn't respond. He could only stare in horror at the grisly trophy.

The young man looked at it, shook his head sadly, and then cast the item off to the side where it thumped against the leg of Connor's roll-top desk. Jonathan brought the crucifix up to his lips, kissed it and let it go. Connor watched as it swung freely from left to right and back. A messianic pendulum. The young man pointed his knife at Connor and once more began to weep. Before Connor could ask him why the tears had started again, the young man lunged at him.

Frantically, Connor turned around and tried to run, but his boots could gain no traction on the curious sand scattered across the floor. He felt a hot hand on his shoulder, and a second later, something terribly cold plunged into his back. Connor tried to breathe, but the air rushed out of his mouth. He sank to his knees and coughed as the chill, foreign object was removed from him. The burning hand guided him to the floor. Connor was rolled onto his back as he struggled to breathe. Jonathan knelt beside him as tears spilled down his pale cheeks. Connor felt fingers work their way into his hair, squeeze and pull down and back. His throat was exposed, and he could see the young man raise up his left hand.

The last thing Conner saw was how the crucifix caught the morning light and glowed within it. The blade of the knife was red with fresh blood.

I should have left it in the wall, he thought. *I should have left the damned thing in the wall!*

The ghost plunged the knife into Connor's neck and sawed at the flesh.

"Look what they make me do," the young man whispered, weeping. "Look at what they make me do."

* * *

Shelter

The glass broke easily, and almost inaudibly.

Ryan knocked out the last few shards which clung to the frame, reached in and unlocked the door. The sun had begun its slow descent, and the air was bitterly cold. The folks at the soup kitchen had warned the homeless crew about how the temperature might get into the teens. Possibly even the single digits. Time to get rid of your pride and find a bed for the night.

Ryan couldn't agree more. But he refused to go to a shelter. *Nope. Better to spend the night in jail,* He thought. Except Ryan didn't want to be in custody either.

Plenty of abandoned houses around. And in New England, the heat was almost always left on. Banks couldn't sell a house with burst pipes. Nobody, not even someone who bought a foreclosure, wanted to deal with flooded rooms. Ryan had broken into plenty of houses before. Not to steal anything. No. Just a place to sleep. Maybe for a night. Sometimes, a week. It all depended on how nosy the neighbors were. And Ryan felt like this house, well, he might make it all through winter in this one. It was at the edge of town on a dead end road. The nearest house was two lots up. And it looked like the people living there were snowbirds, flown south to Florida weathering out the New Hampshire winter. Which was fine with Ryan.

Ryan needed a room without windows, if possible. And if not, well, then a room with just one would be fine. He could cover a single window up and allow himself the luxury of a light after the sun went down. A rare treat when you're squatting in an abandoned house. Yes, things looked good.

He popped the door open, slipped inside with a wide step over the broken glass and quickly closed and locked the door. He knew the empty pane would tip off any cop who took a stroll around the house, but Ryan figured he was safe. Cops usually didn't check on abandoned houses. They had other occupied places and taxpayers to worry about.

With the door closed behind him, Ryan looked around. Not surprisingly, he was in the kitchen. It was barren of furniture and utensils. A fine layer of dust coated the floor and the counters. The old, analog clock set into a yellow stove ticked away.

Someone's still paying for the electricity, he thought with a smile. Ryan moved a few steps forward, spotted a wall sconce and found a bulb in it. He quickly unscrewed it, held it to his ear and shook it.

Nothing.

The filament wasn't broken. *Better and better*, Ryan thought. He moved quickly through the rest of the house. In what must have been the dining room, where an old brass chandelier hung down above a pale wood floor, he found the thermostat. It was an old, round dial job with a mercury switch, and it was set at sixty-eight degrees. He resisted the urge to turn the heat up to seventy, and made his way to a set of stairs. Each step creaked loudly beneath him as he went up to the second floor.

At the top of the landing, he found a bathroom. The toilet flushed, and the water ran from the tap. In a small linen closet, he found a stack of old and tattered towels and sheets. He tucked them under an arm and went through the rest of the second floor. At the back corner, he found a small bedroom with only one window. And it had a shade. The room was empty, but it smelled of pipe tobacco and mints. The brown carpet was worn, except for a rectangle beneath the window.

This is where the bed must've been, Ryan thought, walking to the darker space. He put the old linens on the floor, put the light bulb on top, dropped his backpack beside them and went and opened the closet door. Inside, Ryan found an old overcoat and a small light. It was a children's bedside lamp. There were lions and a lion-tamer on it. The top of a circus tent and a battered cloth shade. He took both out and added them to his collection on the floor.

For the next ten or fifteen minutes, he prowled around the rest of the house. There was a tall linen closet in the hallway, two other bedrooms, and a closed trapdoor in the ceiling, which he ignored. He found a woolen blanket tucked into the back of the top shelf in the linen closet. Ryan also found some old books stacked in a corner of a walk-in closet in what was probably the master bedroom. He was nearly giddy as he brought everything back to the bedroom.

The solitary window looked out over a large expanse of woods which ran out into Pachaug State Forest. Ryan doubted anyone would walk by through the trees and look at the house, but just in case they did, he'd have a sheet doubled up and over the shade.

The bedroom door, he discovered, opened and closed easily, even with a sheet hung upon it. He worked quickly to get the door closed, with the top, and bottom jammed with a pair of old towels. When all of the cracks were covered, and Ryan was in near total darkness, he dug his Zippo out of his pocket and rolled the flint.

The flame burst into life, and he blinked several times as he held it over his head. He looked from the door to the window and nodded in satisfaction. Then, careful not to set the house or himself on fire, he put the bulb into the lion lamp, fit the shade into place, and then plugged the old light into the wall.

When he turned the switch, a soft glow radiated out into the room. *Let there be light,* Ryan thought, letting his Zippo go out. He flipped the cap closed and tucked it away. For a minute, he sat on the floor and enjoyed the feeling of warmth and safety the small lamp spread through the room. Then, with a sigh, Ryan unpacked his bag.

A few cans of beans from the shelter. Several bottles of water. A cheap pint of vodka. Spare socks and underwear. And his sleeping bag.

Ryan smiled at the last item, untied it and then he rolled it out on the carpet where the bed used to be. He took the wool blanket, threw it over the sleeping bag, and then took the old overcoat and folded it into a rough pillow. Ryan hummed happily as he turned his attention to the books he had found. Two of them, were romances. Good old fashioned bodice rippers. Another pair, were westerns by Louis L'Amour. And the last, the last was 'Salem's Lot, by Stephen King.

A grin spread across Ryan's face, and he nodded to himself, pleased. He put the book down on the blanket and then did something he hadn't done in an extremely long time.

He got undressed. He wasn't worried about his boots being stolen. Or his pants. Or his sweatshirt.

This place is safe, Ryan told himself.

He neatly folded each article of clothing and set them in a pile beside his boots. After he had picked up the book, he slipped into the sleeping bag and enjoyed the way the cool nylon felt against his skin. Ryan sighed happily, got comfortable, opened the book and began to read. Thirty or so pages in, he realized he was tired, yawned, and marked the page of the book before he put it down on the floor next to the lamp. He reached out, turned off the light, and rested his head on the floor.

The smell of mint and pipe tobacco was comforting. Ryan smiled, closed his eyes, and let himself relax. He would hear if someone entered the house. Twelve years on the road had taught him how to listen, even in his sleep. He continued to smile as his thoughts drifted. He remembered the meal at the Soup Kitchen. The argument with Slim over the best place to sleep.

"Who are you?" a voice asked.

Ryan opened his eyes, unsure of where he was, for a moment. *The house,* he thought. Then he froze. *Jesus, did someone just talk in here?*

He fought down a wave of fear, remained still and let his eyes roam the darkness. He could barely see the outline of the window, or even the door. *No,* he chided himself. *This is what you get for reading a horror story before bed, dummy.*

"Did you hear me, son?"

There *was* definitely someone in the room. A man. Panic welled up within Ryan's chest and he fought to control it as he realized that the voice hadn't come from the door. It came from the closet. The pipe smell had grown stronger. The closet door swung open, and the floor creaked.

"Son," the man said, a hint of anger entering his voice, "I suggest you start speaking."

Ryan cleared his throat nervously. He had to figure this out. He couldn't run. He was naked in the sleeping bag.

"I was just looking for a place to sleep," Ryan said. *How the hell did he get in the room? How did he get into the closet?*

"A place to sleep?" the unseen man asked.

"Yes, sir," Ryan said hastily. "Just seeking shelter from the weather."

"This is my house," the man said.

"I didn't know anyone lived here, sir," Ryan said, starting to sit up.

"Stay where you are," the man snapped.

Ryan stopped.

"I live here," the man said angrily. "I live here. This is my house!"

"I didn't know," Ryan said. "The place is empty."

"I know it's empty," the man said. "I'm the reason it's empty. Nobody, but me, lives here. Nobody! They can sell it to as many people as they want. I'll chase 'em all off. You understand?"

"Yes," Ryan said.

"You know you're trespassing," the unseen man said.

"I didn't see any signs, sir," Ryan said. He reached out slowly for his clothes.

"Stop moving around!" the stranger yelled. Ryan stopped. *How the hell can he even see me?*

"Now it's bad enough you're trespassing," the man said, a moment later. "But what's worse, is how you took my boy's lamp."

"What?" Ryan asked, confused.

"My son's lamp. His bed light. The lion-tamer, you idiot," the stranger snapped.

"I didn't take it," Ryan said desperately. "It's right beside me. Look."

He reached out, found the light and turned it on. The light, as weak as it was, momentarily blinded him. When he could see again, he turned to the closet and froze. The door was open, and the closet was empty save for a handful of wooden hangers. The sheet still hung upon the bedroom door. The towels were still stuffed around the edges.

"See," the man said, his voice emanating from the closet. "You have my boy's lamp." *Oh, Jesus Christ help me,* Ryan prayed, suddenly terrified. *This place is haunted.*

A floorboard creaked, and Ryan realized the ghost had left the closet.

"You're a thief, and a trespasser," the unseen man snarled.

"I didn't steal the lamp," Ryan said weakly. "And, I just needed a place to stay. Just a warm place to stay."

"A place to stay?" the dead man asked. The floor squealed and a cold sensation bit at Ryan's feet through the woolen blanket and the sleeping bag. "You just needed a place to stay?"

"Yes," Ryan whispered, trying desperately to think of a way to take his clothes and race out of the room.

"A place to stay," the man hissed. The cold spread up Ryan's shins and to his thighs.

"Well," the dead man said softly. "I suppose you can stay here with me."

Cold hands locked around Ryan's throat and squeezed as he screamed. He flailed at the dead man, yet Ryan could do nothing. Stars exploded in front of his eyes and pressure built in his head. His lungs howled for air, and he fought desperately just to free himself of the sleeping bag. As his vision grew black and he dropped his arms to the floor, Ryan finally caught sight of the dead man. He was huge, dressed in an old flannel shirt and a pair of nearly threadbare overalls. There was a pipe clenched between his teeth, the embers of tobacco, orange and bright in the briarwood bowl. Black eyes glinted.

"Yes," the ghost said around the stem of the pipe. "Yes. You can stay with me for a while. I won't rob you of your *shelter.*"

The pressure eased up around his neck and a chill washed over Ryan.

"*Shelter,*" the dead man hissed-and Ryan found breath enough to scream as he was dragged into the closet.

* * *

The Shepherd

For three months, David had listened to his parents talk about the killings.

Two sheep in March. Three in April. Another pair in May. Seven sheep out of forty-three. Not much for some of the bigger farms, but for David's family, seven was a lot.

David lay in his bed in the loft and wondered why his parents didn't believe. At fifteen years old, David knew a lot. And yet, he understood there was a great deal more, he didn't. A rare trait, Ms. Holmes said. He was one of the few students who didn't sass her. She liked how he wanted to learn, and how he loved to read. And because of his politeness, she had happily gotten him the curious books he had requested. The fairy tales about the bad things, the dark things, which hunted men, as well as beasts.

David believed he knew what sought out his father's sheep, just as he learned what had to be done to save them. He doubted Ms. Holmes would have agreed with him, though. As smart as she was, she was still an adult. And most adults didn't believe in fairy tales or boogeymen. David thought of the sheep, the way they'd been torn apart and devoured. Little more than fur and bones had remained.

His thoughts were interrupted as his father came into the house. David peered over the side of the loft and down into the main room. His mother sat by the fire and mended a tear in his pants. He watched as his father stepped over to her, bent and kissed her swiftly. She looked up and smiled. "Did you have any luck?"

"No," his father said, shaking his head. He put his shotgun in its corner to the left of the chimney, took off his light coat, hung it on a hook by the pantry cabinet, and sighed.

"Coffee?" his mother asked.

"I'll get it, Love," his father said. David watched his father get some of the strong, dark, brew the man enjoyed so much. With a grunt, his father took his chair opposite his mother, who put her mending down and looked at him.

"Are you alright?" she asked. He shook his head. "No. I've checked the pasture, made sure the new fence is secure and herded the sheep into one corner. Like every night, we can only hope all of our sheep will be safe when morning comes."

"Isaac," she said, "does anyone know what it is, yet?"

David listened carefully. "No," his father said, "we don't have enough tracks to go by. Some say a wolf, others say a coydog, some overlarge offspring of a dog and coyote. It doesn't matter, though. I just wish we had a way to stop it."

"Perhaps, it will move on," his mother said. "It wasn't here before the end of the year. We can hope it will find greener pastures."

David's father grunted his approval, took a clay pipe from its mug on the mantle and packed himself a full bowl. He reached out, took a match from a small shelf and struck it on the stone of the fireplace. Carefully, he lit the tobacco, exhaled and tossed the match into the fire.

"We can hope," his father finally said. "If it happens again, I'll have to see about hiring the Claussen boy to keep a better eye on the field."

"Could we do it tonight?" his mother asked hopefully.

"No," David's father said, shaking his head. "We don't have enough money to take him on, yet. We can only pray nothing will happen in the next month."

No, David thought. *Nothing will happen after tonight, father.*

With a sigh, David closed his eyes and tried to sleep. It would be time to get up, soon enough.

His parents spoke for a little longer, mostly of concerns for the farm. Whether or not the corn would survive any early rains, if all of the apple trees would continue to produce. The last discussion he remembered was about a raise for Ms. Holmes. Her contract was to be renewed at the next Church meeting.

David awoke to the sound of his mother's cuckoo clock as it called out two in the morning. He lay on his back and heard the steady rhythm of his father's snores and his mother's soft exhalations. David sat up and quietly dressed.

Fear ripped through him as he briefly thought about what he planned to do. He pushed the fear aside, pulled on his sweater and then went down his ladder and descended into the main room. He moved slowly, careful on the fifth rung down since it creaked loudly when weight was placed on its center. David avoided it successfully, saw how his mother and father still slept peacefully and crept to the door. He paused, then silently slid the cross beam out, and unlocked the latch. Again, he risked a glance at his parents.

His father snorted, rubbed his nose in his sleep, and then he dropped his hand back to the bedside. David went to the pantry and eased the narrow door open. He felt around the dim depths until he found the hardwood case which held part of his mother's dowry. Fine cutlery which had accompanied the cuckoo clock on the mantle all the way from Bavaria after his mother and father had married.

Carefully, David set the box on the floor and opened it. From the velvety depths, he removed a long carving knife from its place between a serving fork and a long handled ladle. The handle was dark and smooth, made from the antler of a great stag. The blade caught a faint bit of light thrown by the dulled embers of the fire and shined. For a moment, he felt as though he were a soldier, sword ready, prepared to battle the British. David smiled, and his thoughts fell away.

He returned the case to the pantry with the same care and caution with which he had removed it. Then, he closed and latched the pantry door. David grinned nervously and let himself out and into the night. In spite of it being May, there was still a chill in the air. The sky was cloudless and bright. The stars shined and the full moon illuminated the whole of their land.

In the paddock, the sheep were still on their feet. Their mutters and bleats told him they were still awake, and afraid. David could smell their fear. They knew something was wrong.

Silently, he climbed over the fence, and made his way to them. They were all gathered beneath the tall ash tree which stood in the left corner, and they parted to let him pass through. He whispered soft words to them and ran his free hand through their rough wool. His presence soothed those nearest to him, and the calm they radiated, spread out through the remainder of the small flock.

Soon, he found himself beneath the widespread branches of the ash, and he sat down. The chill of the earth seeped through his trousers, and the cold peace of the tree settled into his back. David sat cross-legged and Indian style, his arms in his lap, the antler handle warm in his hand.

And he waited.

The moon shined brightly and David felt fear and uncertainty burrow into his stomach. It gnawed at the remnants of his meal and sought to eat his courage and determination. The wind shifted and a rank, foul odor filled his nose while the sheep bleated in renewed terror.

It was coming.

And they all knew it.

The sheep pressed close to him and their bodies threw off a level of heat only fear could produce. David tightened his grip on the knife and shifted his position. He unfolded his legs, kept himself low amongst the frightened animals, and crouched down. The moonlight illuminated the pasture, outlined the spilt-rail fence, and the dark creature which appeared at the far wall. It was on all fours and low to the ground. It was neither a coyote nor a coy-dog. Not nearly as large as a wolf, but still David saw it was of a fair size. And intelligent.

David watched as it paused at the fence, head between the rails. Fear raged within him, a storm which threatened to rip his courage away. The terror he felt seemed to feed off of the anxiety of the sheep, but David battered it down. He was the shepherd, the one who protected the flock. David knew he had no choice. He must shield them from the beast, ensure their safety. David swallowed and ignored his sudden, painful desire to flee, and waited.

The wind carried its scent to the sheep and caused the fear to run rampant. The beast waited for the fright and terror to run its course; to make the sheep crazed and ready to run. Yet David's own presence offset the scent, and the lack of panic amongst the sheep caused the creature to hesitate.

Will it come anyway? David wondered. *Will it move on to Old Parchman's farm, or perhaps the Stoats?*

He could only hope so. Yet, it didn't.

Gingerly, almost daintily, the beast stepped through the rail. It advanced and the sheep pressed closer to David. He worried they might crush him, but even as the beast neared them, the sheep gave David and the ash a bit of room.

David ignored the shakes and trembles in his flesh. He fought the numbness as it threatened to rob him of what little courage he had, and he kept his eyes on the monster. It was tall at the shoulder, its fur dark gray with strong white streaks. The eyes were a yellow tinged with black, and each step revealed the powerful muscles on its lean frame. The tail hung low, and the ears were pressed flat against the head. It looked similar to drawings of wolves David had seen in his school book, yet it was far longer and lower to the earth.

At the edge of the flock, the animal stopped. David watched silently as the beast seemed to choose the sheep it would cut out. The one it would devour. And the sheep knew it as well. Their bleating rose to a frenzied pitch, and David wondered how either he or his parents could ever have slept through such a sound. The beast sank lower and prepared to strike. David launched himself forward. The monster paused and straightened up, eyes wide and ears up. The sudden change in its posture was almost comical, and then it realized David was armed. David was fast. Faster than any other child in his school. Faster than some of the young men in town. And faster than the beast which had threatened the flock. As the creature turned and tried to run, a hind leg kicked out on a loose tuft of grass and it was all the advantage David needed.

Two long strides propelled him through all the flock, and he leaped the last few feet. He had the knife in both hands, fingers interlocked as he brought the weapon up over his head. As he crashed into the beast, David plunged the blade down into its back and buried the knife to its hilt between the creature's bony shoulder blades. It let out a terrible shriek, horrifically human in nature as it smashed onto the earth. The beast tried to shake David off, but the boy locked his legs around the animal's narrow midsection.

Behind him, David heard his father yell, and his mother scream his name. The door to their house burst open, and lamplight spilled out as the sheep ran. The animals' frightened screams rang out.

The monster fell to the earth and shuddered. A gasp escaped its mouth and David wrenched the knife free only to plunge it once more. Again and again he stabbed the beast. Blood flew up into the night sky. Vaguely, David became aware of his own screams and as he ripped the blade free, he tasted the sharp and bitter tang of blood in his mouth even as he thrust the blade down into the furred body again.

"David!" his father yelled and in the corner of his eye David saw the man leap the fence. His father was clad only in an old nightshirt and nightcap, the shotgun in his hands. From the open door of the house, his mother ran, lamp held upward as her flannel nightgown flapped around her. Suddenly, his father's broad, calloused hand was on David's shoulder. The man pulled David back with such strength it sent him into a tumble.

"Sweet God in Heaven," his father whispered, cocking the hammers of the shotgun.

"Isaac," his mother hissed as she pulled David close to her. David looked at the beast in the moonlight, yet it was no longer a beast.

It was the naked, bloodied form of Mrs. Parchman, the pig farmer's wife. Her gray and white hair was tousled, a look of frozen horror on her face. She was filthy with mud, her eyes clear and white, and the spark of life gone from them. The antler handle of the silver knife protruded from the woman's back and glowed in the light of May's full moon.

David allowed himself to be cradled in his mother's arms, he shivered as he looked at the giant, pale orb in the night sky, and suddenly felt a terrible, horrific longing.

* * *

The Shortcut

At sixteen years old, Mark LeBlonde wasn't afraid of anything. If he could handle the beat-downs from his father, he could handle whatever the rest of the world decided to throw at him. What he couldn't handle, though, was Stephanie Ural's rejection. She was hot, and he wanted to date her. She didn't feel the same.

Not. At. All. Mark thought.

He cut through the driveway of an abandoned house on Pierce Street, reached the iron fence of the cemetery, and hoisted himself up. With great care, he avoided the points of the metal posts, hooked his foot into the top crossbeam and jumped over onto the grass. The air seemed colder in the cemetery, the night sky darker. Mark ignored them both. He didn't believe in ghosts.

And even if they were real, what could they do to me? he thought.

He stuffed his hands into his pants' pockets and dropped his head down slightly. Anger raced through him and flared up occasionally as he thought of Stephanie and her rejection. He released it each time with a kick to a tree or a wire-mesh trash can placed along the cemetery road. As he passed into the older section near the cemetery's center, he saw a white headstone. The marker leaned crazily to the right and looked as though a strong breeze would knock it over. Mark paused and looked at the stone, and then he smiled.

He left the cemetery road and walked across the grass, taking his hands out of his pockets. The stone of the marker was cold beneath his fingers. He gripped the top of the headstone, the surface pitted and worn from years of exposure, and he pushed. The tendons in his neck strained and his shoulders ached, but Mark continued to press his weight against the stone. With a groan and a strange squeal, the marker went over, and Mark stepped back as it crashed to the ground. He could feel the vibration of it through his feet, and Mark realized he felt great. He felt ... strong. He shook his head, laughed and looked around for another. Half a dozen feet away, another headstone was cockeyed on its wide base, and Mark knew it would go. He stomped over to it, took it in both hands as he had done the other, and shoved it. And while his muscles ached and screamed at the sudden, unexpected effort, the stone went over. Mark let out a triumphant shout.

Forget Stephanie, he told himself. *There are other girls, and this is a hell of a lot more fun than chasing her around.*

Mark nodded in agreement with himself, scanned the rows of headstones and spotted another, a few feet away. In less than twenty minutes, he stood by a tall monument to some long dead soldier and panted. He had managed to push over six stones. The last one had split in two, and it made all of the new aches and pains he felt, worthwhile. He leaned against the monument. The cold of the stone worked its way through his clothes and into his flesh, but it was alright. All of it was alright.

"What are you doing?" a voice asked.

Mark nearly jumped as he twisted around to see the speaker. A tall man, probably as old as his father, stood a dozen feet away and stared at Mark. The guy wore an old uniform.

Probably one of those dumb re-enactors, Mark thought, and he sneered at the man.

"Mind your business, pops," Mark said dismissively. The man took a step closer. "I am minding my business. What are you doing?"

"I'm telling you to get lost. Go back to whatever stupid game you were playing, loser," Mark said, shaking his head.

"Did you knock down all those gravestones?" the man demanded.

"So what?" Mark said, straightening up and crossing his arms over his chest. "So what if I did? What are you going to do? Call the cops? Good luck proving it. I'll just deny it. No witnesses."

Anger flashed over the man's pale face, and he took another step forward.

"What are you going to do, old man?" Mark asked, laughing. "You think you can really handle me? I'll beat you bloody and drag you out onto the sidewalk so everyone can watch you bleed."

"Is that what you think you'll do, young man?" the stranger asked softly.

"I know it is," Mark spat. He sized up the man in front of him and laughed. The man smiled grimly and walked forward. He passed directly through a headstone. Mark blinked. The man continued to glide forward and went through a second stone.

He's a ghost, Mark realized. He turned and ran.

In the darkness of the night, he sped around markers and trees until he reached the cemetery road again. He glanced back once and saw the dead man was just a few feet behind him. Not even running. The man's legs weren't moving anymore, it was as though he was tied with an invisible cord to Mark.

Mark stumbled, caught himself, and aimed for the Kinsley Street entrance.

"Why are you running?" the ghost asked, mockingly. "I thought you were going to fight me? Teach me a lesson like you said?"

Mark didn't answer. He raced through the granite posts which marked the entrance. Another glance back, showed the ghost stopped at the edge, and Mark let out a laugh. But it was cut short by a Camaro. The car smashed into him. Mark couldn't scream. He couldn't even breathe.

In, what felt like, slow motion, he watched the world tumble around him. Buildings spun and Mark realized he couldn't hear anything. The world was silent. He vaguely felt the impact of his body as it crashed into the pavement. Almost as if it wasn't really happening to him.

I just bounced, he thought tiredly. The world racing away from him again. And then he was back on the pavement. He rolled and shuddered and rolled again. Headlights illuminated the road, which he could barely see. A film of red had fallen over his eyes. Nothing looked right. He tried to move his head and found he couldn't. The world seemed frozen, or at least, he was.

Someone's feet came into view. Nike sneakers, pink with black trim and black laces. New, by the looks of them. On the pavement, a dark liquid spread out slowly, and Mark realized he could still smell things. Things like burned rubber and hot oil. A strong coppery scent which he couldn't quite place. And Mark smelled urine, too.

Again, he tried to move, but nothing responded. Not even his toes. The person with the Nike's came to a stop and squatted down. A middle-aged man, wearing jeans and a sweater. A shocked look was frozen on the man's face. Even though the world was red, the man's face stood out in sharp relief. The man, who must have been the driver of the car, had a strong, almost movie-star face. His hair was combed back away from his forehead. He even had a biker's mustache, both sides hanging down well past the man's chin. A single earring glittered in the stranger's right ear. The shock slowly left the man's face, horror and disbelief settling in.

A moment later, the man was joined by another person, a priest. The priest dropped down to his knees, and Mark realized the man was barefoot, shirt untucked and collar half in. More than likely, he had run from the St. Patrick's rectory, which was just a block up.

Mark felt strange as he looked and examined the small bit of the world available to his frozen eyes. The priest was an old man, pale faced with white blonde hair. He was chubby, and he had a look of genuine concern. The priest's lips moved, and he reached out a hand. Mark knew the hand was on his head, but he couldn't feel it. He couldn't feel anything.

I'm dying, Mark thought sadly. *I'm really dying.* He wanted to cry, but he couldn't.

Then, just beyond the man and the priest, Mark saw him. The soldier ghost from the cemetery. The dead man crossed his arms and smiled. Through him, Mark could see the cemetery's iron fence, and beyond that, the small chapel and the office. The man's expression was one of self-satisfaction, as though a job had been well done.

In the silence of his own thoughts, Mark heard another voice and saw, with rising horror, it was the ghost who spoke.

"Did you like your little run?" the ghost asked. Neither the driver nor the priest reacted to the dead soldier. They didn't hear him.

"I enjoyed it," the ghost said, drifting closer. The driver rubbed his arms and in the glow of the car's headlights, Mark saw goose bumps erupt on the man's neck.

"Oh yes," the soldier said, nodding. "Yes, I enjoyed it *tremendously!*"

Mark wanted to close his eyes, to look away, to do anything other than stare at the ghost, but he couldn't.

"Do you know what the priest is doing right now?" the dead man asked. "No. I imagine you do not. He is giving you your last rites. He is preparing the way for your death. And, eventually, you will either descend or ascend. I highly doubt it shall be the latter, however."

The soldier moved a few steps further. Mark watched, both fascinated and horrified at the way the small hairs on the priest's neck stood up at the ghost's nearness.

"I suppose you should have looked before you ran," the ghost said. "Just as I suppose you should not have knocked over those headstones."

Lights flashed on the trees, and Mark knew the police or an ambulance had come. But he also knew he was dying. He could *feel* it. The soldier grinned.

"Yes, you'll be dead shortly. And, if I were kind, I would let you slip away. But you weren't kind were you, boy? No, no you weren't. So I think perhaps you will stay with me for a while. Perhaps, I will educate you on kindness, decency, and *respect.* You see, boy, there is a hierarchy in death, and since you've been a wretched beast of a child, the Angel of Death is in no rush to reap your soul. You'll be mine. Who knows for how long, but for now, your soul is *mine.*"

With the last word, the ghost stepped between the driver and the priest, leaned down and thrust his hand into Mark's chest and squeezed.

Mark felt a tug, and when the soldier withdrew his closed fist, he held something long and silver. It looked much like a length of rope and as Mark felt it being slowly pulled out of his chest, he realized it was his soul.

Mark watched the ghost continue to drag the silver cord out of his chest, past the driver and the priest, whose lips moved in silent prayer. Mark felt his heart slow down, the space between each heartbeat growing longer. The ghost smiled grimly, gave one final tug, and Mark's heart ceased to beat.

Suddenly, he found himself in the soldier's grasp, the dead man dragging him towards the cemetery. Mark, dazed, looked out onto Kinsley Street. He saw a police officer running towards the driver of the car and the priest, both of whom had their backs to Mark.

On the pavement in front them, crumpled and in a pool of blood, was Mark's own body.

"Come, boy," the ghost said sharply, "it's time for your education."

Mark tried to free himself, but the soldier's grip was too strong. Darkness reached out from the cemetery and enveloped him as fear tore a scream from his throat.

* * *

The Ghost Hunters

Pete and Angela Lee were amateur ghost hunters. Pete knew that someday the Travel Channel would pick them up. Eventually, the executives would see their pitch and give it the green light for production.

One day.

Until then, he and Angela were stuck at the amateur level. They both had to keep their jobs at the flower shop.

"Hey, sleepy head," Angela said, poking him in the ribs. "You awake?"

He looked over at her and smiled. "Yeah. Sorry."

"No worries," she said, pulling into the driveway of the house at thirty-three Beech Street. As Angela turned off the engine, a middle-aged man stepped out on the front porch. Pete got out of the car, closed the door and waved politely. The man on the porch, Mr. Dennis Wilson, returned the wave hesitantly before he descended the stairs and walked to greet them.

"Dennis?" Pete asked, extending his hand.

"I am," he said, shaking Pete's hand quickly. "Angela?"

Angela nodded, tucking the car keys into her bag. "How are you?"

"Concerned," Dennis said, his voice tight. "Come on in."

Pete and Angela followed the man into the house. All around them were wine and alcohol boxes stacked three and four feet high in the main room. Through an open door, Pete could see the kitchen, which looked as though it was in slightly less disarray. Dennis stopped by a leather sofa piled with blankets and towels and looked at Pete and Angela nervously. The man cleared his throat, smiled weakly and said, "So, I really hope you two can help us out here."

"We hope so, too," Angela said.

Pete nodded. "Now, Dennis, you said over the phone you just moved into the house?"

"Yes," Dennis said. "Five days ago, to be exact. You know, I should have known. We both should have."

"Known what?" Angela asked.

"Something was wrong with the house," Dennis said. "I mean it was a foreclosure. Place has been empty for decades. We got it for next to nothing."

"And how soon did you start noticing things were a little different?" Pete asked.

"The first night," Dennis said. "My wife Kathleen, and I, both heard a few creaks and groans. Nothing too strange, you know? I mean, the house was built in 1872, so it's bound to make some noise. We've lived in old houses before. But ... this was different," he said, shaking his head

"It went from creaking and groaning," he continued, "to sounding like something was running through the damned walls the second night. We were worried maybe a squirrel or something got trapped, so we called pest control the next morning. The guy came in, said there was nothing. Not a thing! Not any mice, birds, squirrels. Absolutely nothing! He even said it was kind of strange because usually there are at least mice."

"Okay," Pete said. "So, we can rule out animals. Did the noises continue?"

"Yeah," Dennis said. "They got louder the next night. By night four, last night, my wife couldn't take it anymore. She couldn't' sleep. This morning, she went to pack up our two cats, and she couldn't find them."

"Are they outdoor cats?" Pete asked.

"No," Dennis said, shaking his head. "We never let them outside. And all of the windows and doors were closed. We searched all over the place for them. All we found were some fresh scratches in the hall on the floor."

"Did your wife leave afterward?" Angela asked.

"Not until later, because we spent so much time searching everywhere," Dennis said, "but eventually, she left. Last night was the worst. I didn't sleep at all, and usually, I can sleep through anything. It's like whatever is here wanted me to be up. Every time I started to drift off, bam! Something would wake me up."

"I called you guys yesterday because one of the neighbors had seen a segment on you in the news a while ago."

"Are you planning on staying here tonight while we investigate?" Pete asked.

Dennis shook his head vehemently. "No. Oh, hell no! I'm giving you the key. Just lock up in the morning when you're done. Leave it under the doormat for me. My wife and I need to figure out what we're going to do with the house. I think New Hampshire has some sort of law about failing to disclose a haunting, but I'm not really sure."

"I understand," Pete said. "We'll gather as much evidence for you as we can, and we'll document everything we find."

"Please," Angela said sympathetically, "try and get some rest. We'll be in touch tomorrow morning, about nine or so."

"Okay," Dennis said. He dug his hand into a pocket, pulled out a silver house key on a ring and handed it over to her. "Here. Like I said, just leave it under the mat. Good luck tonight."

"Thanks," Angela said, slipping the key into her own pocket.

Dennis glanced around, took his car keys off the sofa, smiled tightly and left the house.

"Sounds pretty active," Pete said after they heard Dennis' car pull out.

"You said it," Angela said as she looked around. "Where do you want to set up the gear?"

"What do you think, make this room our base of operations?" Pete asked.

"Yes," Angela said. "Definitely. Then we can put a kit in the bedroom."

"Hall too, if we can see the scratches left by one of the cats," Pete said, nodding to himself.

"Okay," Angela said, "let's get everything set up and ready to go."

Pete smiled at his wife, and the two of them went back to the car. They pulled the black hard-cases out of the trunk, the bag of batteries, and the bundles of cords. With everything gathered up, they went back into the house, the two of them working together in silence. It took nearly an hour to get each piece up and running. They had motion sensors, audio and visual recorders, Wi-Fi boosters, and a slew of specialized equipment carefully purchased over the years.

By the time the sun had set, Pete was pouring coffee out of the Thermos and into two small cups.

"Thanks," Angela said, smiling at him. She looked at the pair of laptops they had set up. "This should be a pretty good night, if he and his wife were actually experiencing what they thought they were."

"Guess, we'll find out," Pete said, taking a sip of his coffee and wincing. "Still too hot."

"That's why it's steaming," Angela said with a smirk.

"Ha, ha, ha," Pete said sarcastically, as he put his cup down on the small folding table that the laptops stood on. "You're pretty funny."

"Yeah," Angela said, "I know."

They settled down into the relative comfort of their folding chairs, slipped headsets on and prepared themselves for a long night. A single work light stood behind them, casting just enough illumination for them to see and work by.

Time passed slowly. It was typical of most investigations. Pete knew they might see an orb, or perhaps even a power spike on one of the sensors if they were lucky. And he hoped they would be. After several hours, though, nothing had happened. It wasn't unusual, only mind-numbingly boring. Pete couldn't engage in mindless chit-chat or discuss real concerns when they were on a job. He and Angela needed to remain focused on the task at hand.

Eleven edged closer to midnight, Pete finished off the last bit of his first cup of coffee. The drink was cold, but he had nursed it long enough. He knocked back the last mouthful, grimaced at the bitter aftertaste and poured himself another. When he put the Thermos away, a loud noise reverberated through the headphones, and he looked sharply at Angela. Her eyes were wide as she looked closely at her laptop. Pete leaned in and the two of them looked at the display. The noise had originated in the hallway, the motion sensor flashing brightly. Each time the audio sensor's readout spiked, the lights on the motion detector increased their rhythm. Nothing was visible. Not a faint mist or a free-floating orb. Nothing dark except for a deep shadow to the left of the stairs. Even with the infrared lens on the camera, they couldn't see into the shadow, although the claw marks of a cat stood out starkly on the wooden floor.

"Do you think we could adjust the camera and get a better look into the shadow there?" Angela asked softly.

"Yes," Paul whispered. "Be right back."

He slipped his headset off, stood up and stretched his legs for a moment, and then pushed past the heavy tarp they had hung up in the doorway to block the light of their command center. As the plastic sheet fell back into place, he made his way as quietly as possible in the darkness to the hallway camera. His progress was announced by the squeaks and squeals of the old wood floor. Decades of constant travel had loosened boards as well as the subfloor, and the nails no longer gripped as they should.

Finally, Pete made it to the hallway. Everything was dark save for the flashing green lights on the motion sensor. It still continued to read movement in the shadow. Pete paused behind the device. He tentatively extended his hand, trying to see if there was a cold spot.

There wasn't.

With a sigh, he squatted down, adjusted the camera's tripod and slid it a little closer to the corner. While the entire hallway was dark, he could still see slightly. Ambient light from the street beyond, filtered in through bare windows. None of it penetrated the corner. Pete moved the motion sensor and the audio recorder, making sure they both had a clear line of sight into the dark shadow. Something scurried by in the darkness and Pete straightened up nervously. His heart raced, his mouth went dry, and he wondered what the hell it was.

After a moment, he thought it must have been one of the cats, and he called out softly to it. "Kitty. Come here, Kitty."

When no cat was forthcoming, Pete got down on his hands and knees, crawled a little closer to the shadow and called again to the cat.

Bet the damned animal was caught in the walls, Pete thought as he moved further in.

A hiss sounded to his left, in the deepest part of the shadow and he rolled his eyes. The last thing he wanted was to see if there were any band-aids left in the first-aid kit in the car. Cat scratches would not be enjoyable.

"Here, Kitty," he whispered again. And he froze as something brushed his ear. It hadn't been a cat's whisker or even fur. It had been hard, dry and rough.

From the front room, Angela yelled, "What the hell was that?"

Before he could ask what she was talking about, something grabbed his ears, both of them. Stars exploded in his eyes as his head was thrust down to bounce off the floor. He let out a pained moan and collapsed with all the grace of a gutted fish. His ears rang and light burst into the hall, causing him to close his eyes tightly. Hands grabbed his wrists, and he asked in surprise, "Angela?"

Her yell forced him to open his eyes, and a scream of shock and horror was torn from his mouth. Angela was running towards him. She wasn't the one holding onto his wrists. Pete wasn't even sure *what* gripped him. The creature was short and stout, clad in worn, ill-fitting clothes. Its skin was a mottled gray, with spots of dark green, and its head was squat and nearly shaped like a football. It grinned happily at him. Its teeth were disturbingly black and sharp, and there were far too many of them. Hands, which seemed to be far too large for its body, gripped Pete's wrists, and off to the left he saw a small section of the hallway, the dark corner, was open. A small passage extended beyond the wall, the lathing and horsehair plaster were visible.

Several other creatures similar to the first crowded the entrance, watching everything intently. Then the creature began to drag Pete towards the small doorway.

As Pete struggled to free himself from the strange thing's monstrously strong grip, Angela reached them. She paused, only for a moment, before she aimed a kick at the creature's back, her sneaker landing squarely and loudly. The beast let out a shriek and dropped Pete, turning quickly to Angela. Yet even as it did so, she kicked out again, hitting it in the face and sending it sprawling backward.

Shrieks arose from the creatures watching from the doorway, and they came rushing out. They swarmed over Angela, bringing her crashing to the floor. More raced from the passage to grab hold of Pete.

Angela's screams shocked him. His own cries joined hers as hundreds of teeth found his flesh. Pete started to shriek as his clothes were stripped off his body and the hideous things began to eat them. His throat felt as though it would burst from the force of his screams. A hand gripped his right ear and tore it from his head while sharp teeth severed tendons and shredded muscle. Again Pete tried to twist away, but his head was held firm. As he opened his mouth to scream once more, a small hand darted into his mouth and ripped out his tongue.

As Pete and Angela were slowly devoured alive, the camera remained on its tripod, silently recording the gruesome and bloody feast.

* * *

8. This is Gonna Hurt (Short Story)
   http://www.scarestreet.com/Thisisgonna

And experience the full-length novels (150 – 210 pages):
Ron Ripley (Ghost Stories)
1. Sherman's Library Trilogy (FREE via mailing list signup)
   http://www.scarestreet.com/
2. The Boylan House Trilogy
   http://www.scarestreet.com/boylantri
3. The Blood Contract Trilogy
   http://www.scarestreet.com/bloodtri
4. The Enfield Horror Trilogy
   http://www.scarestreet.com/enfieldtri
5. Moving In (Moving In Series Book 1)
   http://www.scarestreet.com/movingin
6. The Dunewalkers (Moving In Series Book 2)
   http://www.scarestreet.com/dunewalkers
7. Middlebury Sanitarium (Moving In Series Book 3)
   http://www.scarestreet.com/middlebury
8. The First Church (Moving In Series Book 4)
   http://www.scarestreet.com/firstchurch
9. The Paupers' Crypt (Moving In Series Book 5)
   http://www.scarestreet.com/paupers
10. The Academy (Moving In Series Book 6)
    http://www.scarestreet.com/academy
11. Berkley Street (Berkley Street Series Book 1)
    http://www.scarestreet.com/berkley
12. The Lighthouse (Berkley Street Series Book 2)
    http://www.scarestreet.com/lighthouse
13. The Town of Griswold (Berkley Street Series Book 3)
    http://www.scarestreet.com/griswold

Victor Dark (Supernatural Suspense)
14. Uninvited Guests Trilogy
    http://www.scarestreet.com/uninvitedtri
15. Listen To Me Speak Trilogy
    http://www.scarestreet.com/listentri

A.I. Nasser (Supernatural Suspense)

16. Children To The Slaughter (Slaughter Series Book 1)
    http://www.scarestreet.com/children
17. Shadow's Embrace (Slaughter Series Book 2)
    http://www.scarestreet.com/shadows
18. Copper's Keeper (Slaughter Series Book 3)
    http://www.scarestreet.com/coppers
19. Kurtain Motel (The Sin Series Book 1)
    http://www.scarestreet.com/kurtain
20. Refuge (The Sin Series Book 2)
    http://www.scarestreet.com/refuge
21. Purgatory (The Sin Series Book 3)
    http://www.scarestreet.com/purgatory

David Longhorn (Supernatural Suspense)

22. Sentinels (The Sentinels Series Book 1)
    http://www.scarestreet.com/sentinels
23. The Haunter (The Sentinels Series Book 2)
    http://www.scarestreet.com/haunter
24. The Smog (The Sentinels Series Book 3)
    http://www.scarestreet.com/smog

Eric Whittle (Psychological Horror)

25. Catharsis (Catharsis Series Book 1)
    http://www.scarestreet.com/catharsis
26. Mania (Catharsis Series Book 2)
    http://www.scarestreet.com/mania
27. Coffer (Catharsis Series Book 3)
    http://www.scarestreet.com/coffer

Keeping it spooky,
Team ScareStreet

37946363R00034

Made in the USA
Middletown, DE
09 December 2016